SHELTER

SANNEKE VAN HASSEL

TRANSLATION BY / *VERTALING DOOR*
DANNY GUINAN

Shelter
by Sanneke van Hassel

Translated from the Dutch
by Danny Guinan

First published in English
by Strangers Press, Norwich, 2020
(part of UEA Publishing Project)

Distributed
by NBN International

Printed
by Swallowtail Print, Norwich

All rights reserved
© *Sanneke van Hassel, 2020,*
published by De Bezige Bij Publishers
Translation
© *Danny Guinan, 2020,*
mentored by Michele Hutchison

Editorial team
Nathan Hamilton, David Colmer,
Michele Hutchison, Bas Pauw and Victor Schiferli

Editorial assistance
by Senica Maltese

Cover design and typesetting
by Office of Craig

Main body text is set using Arnhem,
Headings are set in Nord

The rights of Sanneke van Hassel to be identified as the author and Danny Guinan to be identified as the translator of this work have been asserted in accordance with the Copyright, Designs and Patents Act, 1988. This booklet is sold subject to the condition that it shall not, by way of trade or otherwise, be lent, resold, hired out, stored in a retrieval system, or otherwise circulated without the publisher's prior consent in any form of binding or cover other than that in which it is published and without a similar condition including this condition being imposed on the subsequent purchaser.

ISBN-13: 978-1911343332

Shelter

CONTENTS

ISLAND   5

**JUST LET ME KNOW WHEN
WE HAVE TO PACK**   13

IN OUR STREET   23

PLASTIC MAN   31

strangers press

ISLAND

The world is blue, houses smudged against the dark sky, trees brushing the heavens. A wall of water washes over the windscreen of the bus. Carlos sets the wipers to their highest speed. The car in front of him zig-zags across the road and slows down. He has just enough time to step on the brakes. *Merda*. Is the driver on the phone? Had one drink too many? Don't honk the horn. If this guy gets a fright he might knock down a cyclist or swerve onto the pavement. Luckily, the car takes the next turn into a side street. Hopefully he doesn't have too much further to go.

Carlos rubs a hand over his face. Friday afternoon traffic, oncoming cars flash past, their dazzling headlights helping to keep him alert.

Donkersingel. At the bus stop the doors open with a hiss. One off, two on. Shapes of bins and bicycle sheds are visible through the bare hedges lining the road. Light burns in the windows of living rooms where colourful characters move around on large screens. By the time he gets home his boys will already be fast asleep, their faces peeping out above their dolphin-print duvets. He would like to do more with them, but he's often too tired after work. Then again, on his island the kids never played much with their parents, more with each other. In the late afternoon, when it's not so hot, they emerge from their homes to play football in bare feet. He remembers waiting for his friends, leaning against a wall as the hot wind blew in from the sea, rolling an empty can in the dust under the sole of his foot.

He shivers, the blue sweater of his uniform isn't warm enough. Tomorrow he'll wear a vest as well. And look just like his father, who, from the day he arrived in the Netherlands, always wore a vest under the pastel-coloured shirts he likes to remember him in. A man who had made it, not the clapped-out docker that Carlos and his mother found in pensão Delta when they came to join him a few years later. His room was tiny. Through the walls you could hear the other Cape Verdeans who lived in the building, some temporarily, others for years.

The rigid contours of the nursing home appear out of the twilight. *Akropolis* bus stop. He slows to a halt and waits until an old lady in a beige raincoat has hauled herself on board with the help of the grab handle.

'Good afternoon,' he says. The screen on his dashboard tells him that he is three minutes behind schedule but still he waits, allowing her the time to remove her gloves and look for her purse in her handbag. Her twig-like fingers brush against the card reader.

Ping.

'Welcome on board.'

The lady appears to look through him like he isn't there. Paper-thin skin. Straggly hair. Perhaps she isn't feeling well and is on her way to the newly opened clinic in the hospital up the road. Maybe she just needs all her strength to find herself a seat. A lot of elderly folk who travel this route are barely able to make it to the doors halfway down the bus. Carlos lets them get off at the front if they want.

The lady remains standing next to him. She watches the road with him as he pulls out. In the old days, passengers often stood there chatting with him. Later on that was prohibited. The lady says nothing. Maybe she's lost? Old people have been known to walk out of the nursing home and take the next bus that comes along. Before they know it they've forgotten where they are. If this woman starts behaving strangely, he'll call the police and they'll be on the scene within ten minutes.

A row of large white villas perched on small plots on the water's edge line the road alongside the canal.

Weg en Land. The lady stands sullenly beside him, accompanying him out of town.

As he approaches the cemetery the red light comes on. *Begraafplaats*. He stops. No one gets off. He looks in the mirror. Has someone forgotten their stop? None of the dozen or so people on board moves a muscle.

The lady grips the half-door next to his seat with her thin fingers. Does she have a memory of the canal on their left? Of the fields that used to stretch off into the distance here only a few years ago? Does she see the old polders instead of the new houses?

His sense of longing was always strong, but now that he is almost sixty it has become boundless. Maybe because driving is now second nature to him and he has too much time to think — the colours, the sun, family and half-siblings, the chatter in Creole, *'Tud dret?'*, Everything OK?, a hundred times a day. And the scent of fish, the sickly smell of blood as freshly caught tuna is gutted and chopped. Sometimes he finds himself sitting not at a red traffic light in the middle of town but under the table in his mother's kitchen. The adults jostling one another in search of food and rum, music blaring through the house — table legs and perfectly pressed trousers, a skirt with a leopard-skin print, glistening calves.

Dorpsstraat. The shopping centre is adorned with Christmas lights. People stream out of the supermarket armed with heavy bags and wrapped in warm coats. It's a lot busier here now ever since the new houses went up. Lots of new shops, too. Dubai Style Hair Salon, in curly letters, a kebab shop next door.

He passes the last patches of polder, a few sheep grazing in a long-forgotten field, row upon row of identical brick houses with newly planted trees growing out front. The wide pavements are empty. *Venus. Planetenweg*. The freshly laid front gardens are full of wooden benches, carrier bikes and plastic slides.

A teenager gets on at *Poolsterstraat*. He is wearing headphones over his cap. Carlos can hear the thud of the bass as he squeezes past the old lady. He gives him a nod. People are distant islands, but you never know, they might just notice when you raise a hand in greeting or make a gesture in their direction.

He turns up the radio to banish the silence. 'Happy weeeeeeekend,' cries the deejay and on comes 'Time Is On My Side'. Mick Jagger was still a young man when he recorded that song. If only he knew. Carlos has never met a woman who would come running back to him. Love dies. Lately he has been thinking a lot about his first wife, Trudy, about how she used to laugh and sit on his lap, still a young girl. But they worked too hard, Carlos on nightshifts, Trudy in the flower shop. They didn't manage to have children and he spent more and more of his free time making music with his friends. She would go to see her Dutch family, sometimes for the whole weekend. They divorced after two and a half years.

Many years later, when his mother was seriously ill and he had returned to the island for a few weeks, he met Luana. And he became a young man again. Talking, eating, sleeping, touching. Together with her on the bed in one of the many rooms in the family home, the walls blue, the shutters half-closed. Her body completely relaxed. And always wanting more. That same summer she said she wanted to join him in the Netherlands. One year later everything had been arranged. She'd only been here two months when she became pregnant.

He looks to his right. The old lady — gone. Did she take a seat? He can't see her in the mirror. No one boarded in the ten minutes or less that it took to travel from the new housing developments in Pijnacker to the university. Maybe she decided to lie down, stretched out on two seats, or is hiding somewhere down the back. He's not as sharp as he used to be, the year is drawing to a close, he's not getting enough sun.

It gets busy at the university stop. Lots of students. They board the bus with their bags full of books and dirty laundry. He drives on through town, people getting on and off, cheerful chatter, *here comes the weekend*, the radio sings along. He glances to his right again to see if the old lady has reappeared.

The bus empties at Delft train station. The boy with the headphones gets off as well, his eyes fixed on the ground. He must have seen the old lady. Or maybe not, kids these days, all wrapped up in their own worlds.

Carlos grabs his bag and walks over to the office where two other drivers are sitting opposite each other. They greet him. He tries to remember their names. One is a new recruit who complains a lot, about the irregular shifts, the coffee from the machine. The other driver, a small man who never says much, works the regional routes.

He gets home at nine-thirty. Luana is asleep in front of the TV. *The Voice of Holland*, with the sound turned down. The audience is clapping, a singer shuts her eyes, gripping the microphone with both hands. He goes to the kitchen to heat up a plate of rice with chicken and beans.

After dinner he takes his guitar from the stand. When he starts tuning it Luana wakes up.

'I was looking for tickets.' She sits up. 'Nothing under eight hundred euros. Not yet anyway.'

'Mmm.' He starts playing 'É doce morrer no mar', a *morna* that his mother often sang. Luana searches for flights every day. But they haven't saved enough. And they've had to pay the full fare for the kids for years already. Edson will be starting secondary school in six months' time. He spends most of the day staring at the telephone he got for his birthday. His children are not what you would call real Cape Verdeans. You don't see them playing outside in faded t-shirts. They stay indoors and are always asking for stuff, day in day out. Ed did say recently, however, that he'd like to go and visit his father's island.

He used to go back regularly. But then he only needed one ticket, sometimes two. Dutch girls were always keen to make the trip. What was he like with them? It was all so easy, small talk, laughter, laid-back, his hands on their bum. He looks at Luana as she stands up, her low-cut t-shirt, she has become rounder. Could pull her down beside him now on the couch. Carlos, I'm tired, she would say and then start talking about the tickets again.

On the TV screen a woman with a big head of curly hair opens her mouth. The members of the jury nod in appreciation, one of them places a hand on her heart. Luana takes his plate and glass to the kitchen. Silence. The longer they were together, the quieter Trudy became. Until one day she was gone. He plucks the guitar strings hard, looking for a different rhythm, the sea, the gentle swell, like dancing.

'Ed wants to go to football camp this summer.' Luana has come back to wipe off the table.

'We'll see,' he says.

'If he doesn't sign up on time, there'll be no places left.'

'It'll be all right.'

'I sent you the information.'

She sounds like a Dutch woman. Does he have to check his email for something she could just tell him?

'I'm playing my guitar,' he says.

'OK, I'm going to bed. Ed has to be ready to go at eight. It's an away game.' She fetches a bottle of beer from the kitchen and puts it down next to him. 'Have you taken your pills?'

He nods.

She disappears up the stairs. Luana is a good woman, but she's no girl anymore, not since the kids arrived.

He strums. The music sounds better now that everyone is upstairs. *É doce morrer no mar* — it is sweet to die at sea. The song fills the room, with waves, vibrations, stilling something inside him.

When he gets up it is still dark outside. He hears his family moving around downstairs. The boys' high-pitched voices rise up through the ceiling. He quickly pulls on his dressing gown and goes down. They are sitting at the small table in the kitchen eating white bread with chocolate spread.

'I'm going anyway, Dad.' It is the first thing that Edson says to him. Football camp. The next thing on his list after the telephone. Ed never has to carry heavy buckets of water, not like he used to. And Luana doesn't have to go cleaning at the crack of dawn, like his mother did. They'll never learn to fend for themselves.

'Shut it, Ed.' Luana steps in before things get out of hand.

'Good morning, Edson,' he says. 'Sleep well?'

His son mumbles something in reply.

'Go and get dressed,' says Luana. 'We're leaving in ten minutes.'

The kids' clothes are hanging on the radiator in the hall. Ed's sports bag is already packed. Manuel slides off his stool in his pyjamas and rubs himself against Carlos' leg, a warm, swift little animal.

'Go help your mother.' Carlos runs a hand through his son's curls and pours himself a cup of coffee. After he has sat down at the big table in the living room, Luana brings him a sandwich and a glass of water, along with the white pot from the sideboard.

He waits until they have left and the house has gone quiet before taking his pills. He feels himself becoming more relaxed. He looks at the salmon-coloured wallpaper, the colour of the houses on his island. A chain with a crucifix that belonged to his father hangs from the clock above the couch. The clock hasn't worked in years. Unlike Carlos' heart, which is still ticking. He washes down a pill with a mouthful of water. The ever-present fear that it will return, that awful pounding, the feeling of being chased after, of suffocating.

'You will need to have a check-up every three months,' the specialist had told him. That was six months ago, on a sunny morning in June. 'The operation was a success, but you will have to keep a close eye on it.'

Luana had started crying. She pushed him away. But it wasn't about him. It was about their island. When she had left São Vicente to follow him, he had promised her they would return, when they had saved enough money, as soon as possible. Back to his mother's house. Back to the bodies they had twelve years ago. With the tins of mint-green paint she had already bought and the flatscreen and the couch swing she wanted to order. Who would ever think of taking a couch swing to an island? But now they would have to stay here. For the children. For the heart specialist. He drums his fingers on the plastic tablecloth. That's just the way it is.

Saturday morning, the traffic is light. He takes the tram to the depot. The tram driver nods a greeting as he climbs on board. He does so from inside a glass cabin, a security measure introduced a couple of years ago. There are five men waiting in the cafeteria. A young driver is handing out slices of cake, 'Left over from my birthday.' Johan from Carnisse, who started working here around the same time as Carlos, is holding court. He had the early shift on the 32, which goes straight through town. A gang of teenagers on their way home after a night out began throwing beer cans around the bus. Johan pulled over and rang the emergency services, but before they arrived one of the youths threatened to kill him. Verbally, at first, but then he drew a knife. 'I got the shock of my life,' says Johan. He could feel the blade. 'I thought to myself: well, this is it then.' He says it twice.

'Take care,' Carlos says, placing a hand on his shoulder before walking out of the room. Don't dwell on what might go wrong, otherwise you'll never get anywhere.

The buses, which have all just been cleaned, are lined up in the car park. At first he had felt a great sense of freedom, driving around in a brand new bus on different routes and in different shifts. When he started he had figured he would be able to retire at fifty-seven. Then he would go back. There were a couple of bus routes in Mindelo that he could drive for a few *escudos*, just for the fun of it, on bumpy streets and bad roads in a big old broken-down bus.

He hangs up his jacket and settles in behind the steering wheel. After the early retirement scheme was scrapped, the government raised the retirement age. And that's when his heart gave out. 'We have a good life here, too,' he had said to Luana when they got back home from the hospital. 'You just need to adapt and be grateful.' She had said nothing, afraid that he might lose his patience with her, might become agitated, afraid of his heart, afraid of hurting him.

He shuts his eyes, *é doce morrer no mar*, and drives out the gate of the depot. The tarmac is gleaming, it rained last night. The dry air, the strong wind, the rough sea beating against the black rocks, big waves crashing onto the Praia Grande and the sand turning dark. The traffic is flowing smoothly. He'll have to slow down to stay on schedule. He stops for a little longer at the nursing home. The old lady might get on here, with her cold eyes. He expects her to climb aboard. He will expect her each time he stops here now, standing there at his side, like she's fencing him in.

Warmth, on his face, rays of sunshine pierce the pale grey sky. The square with the fountain that never held any water. From where they often had to retrieve the ball, first by jumping over a low wall. The house on the square with the pale blue walls was sold. His grandma died alone, in a room full of strangers, all of her children overseas.

'Hey driver, are we going to move or what?' A fat man in an orange t-shirt has stood up, hands cupped around his mouth.

He steps on the gas and they drive on. Along the canals, along the dike. Along the edge of the city.

As they approach the cemetery a man stands up. Carlos guesses he must be around thirty. 'Thank you, driver. Have a nice day.' He has extremely blue eyes and is holding a bunch of daffodils in his hand, bright yellow in the light that streams in through the windscreen.

Carlos touches two fingers to the side of his head in salute.

After he has driven the route twice, he has a five-minute break. Halfway. At *Berkel Westpolder* he parks the bus and walks over to the drivers' hut. The handful of sheep out in the field are standing with their rear ends facing him. The sun is struggling to break through. Before he enters the hut, he leans his head back and allows the raindrops filling the sky to fall on his face. It is the sea, and it is everywhere.

JUST LET ME KNOW WHEN WE HAVE TO PACK

When the Johnsons told us in spring that they were planning to move house, we weren't exactly surprised. We had heard crazier ideas from them before. Not long after they came to live on our street and had finished renovating their house — complete with marble tiles in the hall and a rain shower in the bathroom — they told us they were thinking about 'moving to Berlin for a while'. That was on a summer evening, five years ago. Flip and I were sitting in their bright, newly painted living room. The lamps were lying unplugged in a corner, still neatly coiled in their own wires. The conversation had gone quiet and we were all looking at the children, who were busy playing with Playmobil on the floor. Berlin, we mumbled to ourselves. The windows were open, sunshine blazed in through the recently restored leaded panes and Ben and Anita carried on fantasizing about where they might move next.

Their two children went to the same school as ours and they liked it there. When we asked what kind of school they would be going to in Berlin, the question was breezily dismissed.

'If you're a professor, you are allowed to educate your own children,' said Ben, and Anita nodded in agreement. 'Or they could go to the international school, which is a good idea these days anyway. It won't take them long to learn English.' That settled the matter as far as Ben was concerned and he turned his attention to pouring the wine, a ritual he carried out with studied solemnity. Sometimes he served a wine with no label, self-bottled, which he would decant with great care; another time he would present his latest find from an obscure French winery.

There was always something to celebrate when Ben and Anita were around. Five years on from that summer evening, the cause for celebration was their decision to 'move to the country', as Ben referred to it himself. Berlin had long since disappeared from the radar and they now had their eye on a small country house in the middle of the Netherlands with its own grounds bordering a forest.

'It just came along by chance,' he said.

Flip gave him a disbelieving look. In my head I could hear him say that the air was no cleaner there than it was in the city, that you would have to move to the Frisian Islands to find that kind of space and fresh air, but he held his tongue and just drummed his fingers on the armrest of a new Gispen chair.

'Imagine that,' was all he could muster, so I asked Ben, 'Have you already arranged everything with the bank?' We had to be sure it wasn't just another one of their whims before taking the trouble to offer our opinion.

'What? Have you told them already?' Anita had returned from the kitchen and was standing in the middle of the room holding a plate of celery sticks. The whole Johnson family had recently started with a paleo diet, and what they were allowed to eat was based on what people ate back in prehistoric times. Bread, sausages, crisps, spaghetti and sweets were all off-limits, but alcohol wasn't. Later on that evening Ben produced his homemade limoncello. Easy-as-pie to make, he said, and we really wanted to believe him.

As night fell outside, we raised our glasses. We listened to their plans and dreamed their dreams for a moment, too. Of course, we could have chosen to be very critical of our friends, but we knew how difficult it all was — the daily grind of raising children, watching your own parents grow old and having a job that wasn't quite as interesting as you made it out to be. We knew, too, how important it was to dredge up your mud-caked dreams every once in a while and rinse them off again, however laborious that seemed.

We talked about our kids, as well as the extravagant lifestyles of our parents, who were from the generation that went on holiday far too often and spent the rest of their time in restaurants and playing golf and tennis. We sang the praises of the lemon-marinated celery and the pan-seared lamb and slipped our children a few extra crackers.

Later, over coffee, and with the children playing football out on the street, which made for easier conversation, we allowed ourselves to become more wistful. Flip sat staring into space. He had known Ben and Anita for a long time; they belonged to that very rare breed of friends with whom you didn't have to make an appointment weeks in advance, but who were always game for a quick cycle around town in the evening, staying out far too late even when they had to be up early the following morning, skipping out to attend the opening of an obscure gallery or catching a gig by an unknown band in a cellar on the outskirts of town.

'It all happened so fast,' explained Anita. The youngest, a girl, took the news badly, 'the tears literally erupted from her eyes'. Their son had merely shrugged his shoulders. 'Just let me know when we have to pack,' he had said, before switching from stoic resistance to computer game in the blink of an eye. '*Clash of Clans*' said Anita. Her son, like ours, lived in a world of bellowing armies, besieged fortresses and a cast of cartoon characters that carried out his every command.

The removals van arrived at their front door during the first week of the summer holidays. We hadn't seen much of each other recently, maybe we had even been unconsciously avoiding them because we figured we wouldn't be able to depend on them anymore, that we would have to go and find ourselves some new best friends. The evening before they left we had them over for dinner one last time. Instead of cooking a farewell meal worthy of the occasion, I threw a pasta salad together using whatever I could find in the back of the fridge. The kids were being impossible; our youngest wouldn't stop screaming and, despite our repeated pleas, exhortations and warnings, the oldest continued to shoot arrows at us from behind the couch.

Ben and Anita couldn't stop talking about their new house, which they were planning to give a complete makeover. There were apple trees at the back of the garden. 'With real apples growing on them,' Anita told us more than once. We nodded distractedly, more concerned with having survived another school year in which the kids had done reasonably well and we had managed to stop falling deeper into debt. Country houses with apple trees were simply beyond our powers of imagination.

The next day we tried to make up for our feeble attempt at dinner the night before. We cycled to their house around noon on Saturday. The weather was warm and grandma had picked up the kids earlier that morning so that we could finish off some work and plan our summer holiday. Ben had already left, he had a project in Amersfoort that required him to work weekends. Anita walked around the empty house gathering up the last of their things into a big blue Ikea bag. I couldn't tell whether she was fighting back the tears or not. She seemed tense and kept her sunglasses on the whole time. I helped her clean out the rooms. They had sold the place for a tidy sum. Now that it was empty you could see just how pristine everything was: the paintwork, the walls all newly plastered only five years ago. The Johnsons weren't leaving much trace of themselves behind. None of the neighbours turned up to say goodbye, maybe they hadn't been living here long enough for that. Or maybe their friends and neighbours didn't even know they were moving. They would return at the end of the summer holidays and stare in wonder at Ben and Anita's house, now a students' residence with a pile of bikes parked out front. A rich businessman had bought the place for his daughter. She and her girlfriends would soon be enjoying the rain shower and using Ben and Anita's lovely kitchen to make their indefinable student food.

Flip picked one of the removal boxes still standing in the hallway and slipped in a bottle of champagne that the Johnsons would find when they were unpacking. We hugged Anita, high-fived the kids, who continued playing football out on the road until the last moment, and then they all piled into their old Audi and drove off.

I had always liked their street, but on this hot summer day all I could see was the empty parking spots and the parched weeds growing out of the sidewalk. I saw how shabby our neighbourhood looked, how there was not enough green and too much run-down social housing. I also saw that Ben and Anita had figured this out long before we had.

We didn't have much contact with each other during the following school year. I'm not a great one for calling on the phone and Flip doesn't like planning too far ahead. That autumn, when we were on our way to a party in Utrecht, we decided to stop by with a bunch of flowers.

Anita remained standing in the doorway and didn't invite us in immediately. We should have called, I had said so to Flip, but he was sure it would be OK. While we were busy reacquainting ourselves with each other on the doorstep, the kids slipped inside, eager to explore their old friends' new stomping grounds. Anita had lost weight, she was wearing a white jumpsuit and looked quite glamourous. More glamourous than I remembered her, in any case, maybe because of her new environs.

They were still busy renovating, Anita told us, and Ben was away in London a lot. 'Come in,' she said eventually, but none too enthusiastically. 'There's a lot of work to be done yet.' She walked ahead of us like a real estate agent showing an obviously uninterested couple around, dutifully opening doors and flicking light switches. Everything in the house was white — the walls, the furniture, the rugs on the floor. We sat down on the enormous couch. I found myself wondering what she meant by 'work to be done' — tidy up a few loose electricity wires perhaps? Remove the last bits of masking tape?

'And how are you doing?' Anita sat down opposite us, placing a bowl of peanuts beside our glasses of wine.

We told her about work, about the children, their new teachers, how they were getting on at school sports and judo, about our parents, Flip's father being operated on again for the umpteenth time, and my parents' trip to Uzbekistan. Anita didn't say much. She went to the open kitchen to fetch a new bottle. She didn't seem all that steady on her feet. 'Champagne anyone?' She rummaged around in the fridge and pulled out a bottle with a pink label.

I asked her where the children were.

'With Ben,' she said, leaning against a door that probably led to a garage or a utility room. She disappeared through the doorway and came back holding a tin of sardines triumphantly above her head.

'As they say, half a loaf is better than none.'

In the meantime, Flip had gone over to the window to look out at the garden. Our children were swinging from a tree, the grass hadn't been mowed in a while. Anita sat down again and placed the bottle, the sardines and a packet of crackers on the table. She looked exhausted.

'You can use the same glass.' I slid my wine glass over to her.

The kids were shouting loudly outside.

'They're fighting,' said Flip, trying to prise open the sliding doors with his fingers.

'There's no key, you'll have to go out the front,' said Anita. She had cut her finger opening the tin and was licking her thumb. Blood dripped onto the white table and she stared at it, a look of satisfaction on her face.

'Wow, look at the colour,' she said, drawing the blood in a red streak across the table with her finger.

'Let me do that...' and I tidied up the crackers on the table. Anita hadn't brought a plate or chopping board from the kitchen, which was very unlike her. Her shoulders began to shake.

'He's gone.'

'Ben...' I stammered.

She nodded her head fiercely.

'Oh no...'

'He's living in a friend's apartment in Amsterdam. He couldn't stand it here anymore. He said it was too quiet for him and he kept hearing voices in his head.' She uncorked the champagne, the cork hit the ceiling and landed limply in the white deep-pile carpet under the coffee table.

'He kept on getting up during the night to check that the front door was locked. He would wander around the house and sometimes go outside in the middle of the night to do God only knows what. He said he felt the walls were closing in on him and that we weren't each other's keepers anyway. Maybe he went out walking in the forest. On one occasion he took the car and came back with his shoes soaking wet.'

Whereas a moment before she had been crying and seemed very confused, she told this story now with a certain kind of glee. Then, suddenly, she stopped. 'Yes,' she said. 'Yes, life is no Russian fairy tale... but then again, maybe it is a Russian fairy tale... Did you know that a lot of fairy tales are based on real-life stories? Take Hansel and Gretel, for example, the two children who go walking in the woods and discover the witch's gingerbread house: a few hundred years ago many children were orphans and there was a lot of hunger.'

'That story is by the Brothers Grimm... Why did you say a Russian fairy tale?' I asked.

'Those are the cruelest kind.' Anita laughed loudly. They hadn't hung any curtains yet and her laughter bounced off the white walls and the enormous windows that looked out onto the garden.

Flip was sitting on the edge of the couch, drinking quickly from his glass. 'Is Ben looking after the children?' he eventually managed to stutter.

Anita nodded. 'My babies,' she said, her voice breaking. 'I hear them the whole time when they're not here.'

A noise sounded from the hallway, was it the front door? Anita put two sardines on each cracker and seemed to perk up all of a sudden.

'My mother always had a tin of these in the house,' she said, 'several tins, in fact. "You never know who might drop in," she would say.' She put a cracker in her mouth. 'Oops, "guests first, Anita."'

From the hall came the sound of children's voices and Ben's too.

'Shoes,' I heard him say. The door flew open. Ben stared at us and we stared back at him.

'Flip, Katleen, what a surprise.' He shook hands with us and then, after a moment's hesitation, kissed us both twice on the cheek.

'Did I miss anything?' He ignored Anita, and when the kids spotted our children out in the garden they ran past her without saying anything.

Anita stood up and spread her arms. 'Benny boy, you're back.' She gave him a kiss, which he didn't seem very keen on, and then tried to push an olive between his lips. He turned his head away and the olive landed on the shaggy carpet.

'Benny boy...' she sighed with a Marlene Dietrich heaviness to her voice, before swinging an arm theatrically around his shoulder. He pushed her away so roughly that she almost fell on top of Flip and had to do her best to keep her balance by grabbing hold of the couch.

'Good, you already have a drink, I see,' said Ben. He went to the kitchen to get himself a glass. Children's voices sounded from the garden, and you could immediately tell that there was trouble brewing out there. No one moved.

Anita straightened her jumpsuit and undid the top button.

'I had just magicked you away,' she said to Ben. 'You were living in a flat in Amsterdam.' She smiled. 'Darling, it was hilarious.'

He filled his glass to the brim with champagne.

'We were in the neighbourhood,' Flip said to Ben.

'Of course, of course. You're always welcome.' Ben drank his glass down in one gulp.

'Nice house,' said Flip.

'Indeed,' said Ben, and then paused for a moment. 'It hasn't been easy, the renovations went on and on, I was very busy at work and it took Anita a while to settle in.'

'How is work going?' I asked.

'I've got a lot on, abroad as well as here,' he said, 'but Anita hasn't been able to find anything for herself, unfortunately, although I don't think she really knows what she wants yet, either.'

'Oh, Anita… she has plenty to do, don't you worry,' said Anita, mimicking a child's voice. 'Anita has lots of shopping and cooking and washing and cleaning and painting to do, as well as making time for herself. She has the gym to go to and the beautician and the gardening club and the school library, and she should really be looking after the garden, too, but she doesn't.'

The children came in carrying a plate covered with leaves on top of which they had arranged a pile of fresh walnuts.

'Fresh walnuts, the real thing,' said Ben. Our youngest went dutifully from one adult to the next and we each picked a greasy, wrinkly specimen. Anita took off one of her pumps and used it to crush the nut.

'Mum…' said her eldest son and her daughter ran to the kitchen to fetch the nutcracker.

Ben showed us how to remove the skin from the nut. 'A walnut tree in the garden helps keep the mosquitoes away,' he said.

Anita tried to get her daughter to sit on her lap, but she wanted to join her friends instead who were cracking nuts on the big bean bag in the corner.

'Yeuch!' cried our children and they spat the nuts out onto the sparklingly clean floor.

Ben and Anita were now ignoring each other completely, and they had also stopped enquiring as to how we were doing. The doorbell rang and echoed through the house.

'You're not expecting anyone, are you?' said Anita.

'We really should be going.' I picked up my handbag from the floor. 'We were actually on our way to a party.'

Ben checked the calendar on his phone. 'Nothing…' he said and stood up.

Through the open doors we could see a large truck standing in the driveway. A man wearing a yellow and red t-shirt was handing Ben a delivery docket.

'It's the outdoor kitchen,' Ben said from the hall.

'I thought you'd cancelled that,' said Anita when he came back in brandishing the docket.

'I ordered it especially for you.' You could hear the cynicism in his voice.

'Need any help?' asked Flip.

'Yes, please,' said Ben. 'If we can get the box up onto a dolly, we'll be able to roll it around to the back of the house.'

The kids dashed out the door after the men. I stood up. Not just to gather up the nutshells from the floor, but also because I didn't think I should drink any more. Even though, given the circumstances, another drink seemed like the better option.

Anita lit a menthol cigarette. I didn't know she had started smoking again. Outside the men were busy cutting the cardboard packaging off the outdoor kitchen, revealing a big, bright red contraption.

'Are you OK?' I asked.

'What do you think?' she said. She stood up quickly and walked to the kitchen, her walk no longer unsteady but determined instead, and plucked a shopping bag from the closet under the sink.

'Come on,' she said, 'let's go and get some meat to throw on that ridiculous thing.'

A while later we found ourselves in the town's huge supermarket. Anita walked around giving orders; she would choose the meat and I was sent off in search of French bread and vegetables. I was glad the situation was back to normal, or at least seemed that way, and did what I was told like an obedient child. When we had left the house, Flip was tearing up the cardboard like a madman. He and Ben had probably finished setting up the outdoor kitchen by now, complete with compulsory cans of beer. The kids had no doubt vanished inside again to play a computer game, their four heads around a single iPad.

Anita had combed her hair and put on some lipstick in the car and was now standing at the meat counter exchanging greetings with the locals. I checked my watch, it read half-past five. We could still get to Utrecht by nine-thirty, the kids were old enough to stick it out until eleven just this once.

Anita and I drove back through countryside that was no longer really countryside but full instead of mansions, bungalows and nameless industrial buildings.

She rolled her window down: 'Just wonderful, all that fresh air, the trees.'

'Yes,' I said. 'I'll never be able to convince Flip to leave the city, but if I could...'

'It takes some getting used to,' she said. 'But we were never able to find what we were looking for back in the city. Ben and I both need space, our own place where we can grow, as well as space up here,' she said, pointing to her head, 'and that's easier when there's lots of room, and silence too.'

I thought of the green olive that she had tried to push between Ben's lips earlier.

'We have promised each other to go out more often, for a bite to eat, dancing, a festival every now and then. We're only an hour from Amsterdam.' She had a worried look on her brow. Or maybe it was just a wrinkle, like me she was acquiring a sizeable collection of fine lines around her eyes.

A deathly silence hung over their street. Everyone was probably around the back on their patios. Or maybe they were all gone, to the tennis club, their boats or their holiday homes.

A heron strutted over to the little round pond in the middle of the front garden.

'There are loads of them around here,' said Anita. 'A few days ago I saw one swallow a frog whole. Gulp. Down in one.'

The heron turned its head fractionally. Then it spread its wings and flew off with short, powerful strokes until it was high above the trees.

We turned into the Johnsons' driveway. I got out of the car and bent down to pick some weeds that were growing between the flagstones. I could see myself living here. Walking the dog, seeing two or three patients and then pruning the vine before hopping into the car at two-thirty to go and pick up the children. After all, I was the main breadwinner in the family, Flip would have no choice but to tag along. I hid the weeds in a potted plant. Carrying the bag of meat, I followed Anita into the house.

IN OUR STREET

It must have been during springtime. The rowan tree in front of our house was just starting to show its first grey-green leaves. I was standing at the window. A couple of seconds earlier I had heard a loud bang, followed by a muted cry.

'Don't look,' I said to the children, who were building Lego houses on the floor, before running to the window. A black scooter lay on its side on the street. A young man was standing next to it with his hands on his knees, moaning. He was slight of build, had dark hair and was wearing a white tracksuit top. Moroccan, I figured.

As I am writing this, I think: a Dutch person of Moroccan descent, not a Moroccan, before realising that I should just write 'Dutch' because that's where we're at these days — which doesn't make it any easier, as a writer, when you are trying to provide a quick impression of a character.

But imagine that it is not the writer's opinion that matters but only what the main character — a 47-year-old female author with the best of intentions — was thinking. She went to the window after hearing a loud noise and, based on hair colour, clothes and scooter, thought she saw a Moroccan out on the street.

On the pavement across the road, two little boys stood watching the man nervously, petrified even. I reckoned he was no more than twenty-one. And really pissed off. A football lay on our side of the street. The boys had more than likely hit the scooter while having a kickabout.

The man raised a fist at the kids. They stood motionless on the pavement, like they had been stuck there with superglue, the kind I used to repair almost everything that needed fixing. Superglue and cable ties — the stuff that kept our house from falling apart.

I decided to go out and have a look.

'Stay here!' I instructed my children. 'You can watch TV,' I shouted over my shoulder when I was halfway down the stairs, to make sure they wouldn't follow me. I didn't want them witnessing any swearing or fisticuffs, if it came to that. I wanted my children's world to be a peaceful for as long as possible, free from confrontation and violence. I ignored the fact that domestic issues probably did more damage than any street skirmish and that my eldest son spent most of his time firing a machine gun on his PlayStation. I let a lot of stuff go back then. In retrospect, my skills as a parent, as a human being even, turned out to be limited.

I opened the front door.

Nikola, the skinny little son of a Croatian mother who lived down the street with her parents, pointed at his friend: 'He did it.'

The other kid's eyes were wide with fear. He had a kind, round face. He was black, but not as black as the Surinamese family two doors down who for years, and to my eternal shame, I had mistakenly thought were from the Caribbean. Until last summer, that is, when the father died and a crowd of people spent several days out on the street in front of the house armed with bags full of food and drinking cognac from plastic cups. When I went to offer my condolences I was immediately invited to the funeral. 'And, *mi gado*, a Surinamese funeral is a real party,' the daughter had said.

Was Nikola's friend from Africa, maybe? And what did I know about Africa anyway, apart from the fact that it is the world's second largest continent? In any case, this little boy was probably Dutch too, or a *Rotterdammer* at least.

Now I think: what does it matter where all these people and their ancestors come from? At the time, however, in terms of the expectations and behaviour of the female lead in this story, it did matter. The story is character-driven, after all, meaning that the plot is largely dependent on how she develops as a person.

I tried to stop the situation from getting out of hand. Of course, I would have done the same if it had involved two white kids from the neighbourhood, but somehow I felt a greater sense of responsibility in this particular situation. As if I was trying to convince the whole world that we were all capable — young, old, all cultures — of living together peacefully.

Cursing loudly, the young man lifted his scooter up off the road. There were dirt marks on his tracksuit top and his jeans were ripped, or was that just the latest fashion? Apart from a slight dent and a few scratches, the scooter looked brand new.

'Are you OK?' I asked.

'It's fucked,' he said.

'I know, even a little damage can be costly.' It's usually best to display some empathy when someone is hopping mad. 'Are you all right? Have you hurt yourself?'

'My leg is fucking stiff.' He examined the side of his hand, which was badly scraped, and then, like a mad dog, his eyes shot to his left, where the children were standing. 'Can you not watch what you're fucking doing?'

The kids tried to make themselves small. Two shell-less, neck-less little tortoises, their heads withdrawn.

'It wasn't my fault,' squeaked Nikola.

'Oh no? Then whose was it?' said the man. 'Santa's?'

'Maybe we should go get your mother?' I walked down to the Croatian neighbours' house with Nikola trailing behind me. He was wearing a red tracksuit with matching bumbag. A few days previously I had seen him in a blue version of the same outfit. Would his mother be in? Perhaps only his grandparents were home and I didn't know whether they spoke Dutch or not. 'Hey,' was all the old man ever growled at me whenever I walked by. Grandma, who I sometimes saw emptying a bucket of water into the gutter — she was the only person on our street who still scrubbed the doorstep — might offer a curt nod.

Nikola's mother was a sharp-tongued woman who was in the habit of reprimanding her son from the doorway of their home. She spoke excellent Dutch, especially when you took the army of swear words she had at her disposal into account. You could spot her a mile away thanks to her beetroot-red hair. She often came home very late. Which was a regular source of gossip. Some said she worked in a nightclub or lapdance bar. But maybe, I thought to myself as we stood there waiting at the door, she just worked at the airport or in a gym that stayed open until late.

She opened the door. 'Now what have you done?'

Nikola looked at her with large, innocent eyes and pointed at the scooter: 'He fell,' he squeaked before turning to look at me, and I dutifully began to explain what had happened.

'Boys will be boys,' said his mother.

I knew from previous incidents that this was her standard reply whenever something went wrong, like when her son let the air out of the tyres on our bikes or insisted on kicking a ball against a neighbour's garage door until he came storming out in a rage.

I nodded my head and said that the children hadn't meant any harm, of course, but that the scooter was damaged. 'Bit of a nuisance,' I said, 'but I'm sure we can sort it out.'

'Hmm,' said Nikola's mother. She followed me over to the scooter, her pom pom slippers click-clacking on the pavement. As we passed my house I looked up. No children's faces pressed against the window, the TV was doing its job.

'Completely fucked.' The man pointed his index finger at the kids, like he was aiming a gun.

Nikola's mother grabbed her son by the ear: 'I told you, you little brat: no playing football in the street.'

'Complete write-off,' said the young man.

'Oh, it's only a scratch.' She let go of the ear with a caustic whip of her hand. 'Nothing that can't be fixed. The Turk, he'll repair it in no time. For a few euros.' She shrugged and turned to me: 'They can really exaggerate sometimes, these youngsters. Unbelievable.'

'You'd better get it sorted,' said the man. 'And if I were you,

I wouldn't wait too long,' he added, shaking his right hand dismissively. The scratch was bleeding slightly, he might have got dirt in it.

'Can I get you something to clean your hand?' I asked, even though I was reluctant to leave the scene.

'Ridiculous carry-on,' hissed Nikola's mother. She turned to her son and raised her hand: 'What did I tell you: no football on the street!'

'I didn't do it.' Nikola ducked to avoid the blow. 'It was him.' He pointed at his friend, who by now had withdrawn completely into himself. The way a child can convince himself that he doesn't exist, can wish himself into non-existence, can act like he doesn't exist at all, and for a moment almost succeed in doing so.

'What's your name?' I asked him.

'Bilal,' he whispered.

'Bilal,' I said, 'maybe you should go get your mother, too. Then we can all sort this out together. Do you live nearby?'

He nodded.

'Off you go.'

Keeping half an eye on the man, Bilal set off running. To his mother, I hoped, though I was more worried about whether he would come back at all.

Whenever I'm teaching a writing class, I advise my students to keep the number of characters in their short stories to a minimum. Otherwise the story becomes too crowded, making it difficult for readers to really get to know the characters. And that's how my life has been these past few years. A free-range henhouse full of chickens scurrying to and fro and cackling incessantly. And not a single one you can get close to.

'He won't be coming back,' said the man.

'Yes he will,' I said. 'We all know each other around here. Our children play together all the time.' Which wasn't true. My own children said they found it too rough out on our street and they refused to go to the playground down the road unless I went with them, which I always did, never knowing whether I was doing the right thing or not. The rough and tumble of the street was nothing new and what they really needed was to learn to fend for themselves. On the other hand, I couldn't deny the fact that the children in the playground were almost always screaming at each other, that they had thrown my son's jumper in the bin, and that a nine-year-old girl from the neighbourhood had recently been kicked repeatedly by a four-year-old boy after being instructed to do so by his older brother. Intervention helped briefly, until the trouble flared up again. I'd read a book called *Respect — 99 Tips For Dealing With Kids & Street Culture*, but it had only given me a better understanding of why my children didn't want to play outside.

'Where does your friend live again?' I asked.

'Down there, next to the playground on the corner.' Nikola pointed towards the next street down from ours across the intersection. I was fairly sure I knew which house he meant. The one on the corner of a block of council houses with the dark blue door and permanently drawn curtains. Next to the front door, a sumac tree was growing out of an enormous bush against which a couple of bicycles had been propped. Whenever I took the dog out at night I often thought about giving the bush a trim. Just to cut it back a little, nothing too severe.

Sometimes I saw a man standing on the doorstep wearing a large cloth wrapped around his waist and sandals with no socks, even in winter. He was joined every now and then by some other men, all wearing the same long tunics. On one occasion I saw them smoking sweet-scented cigarettes. One morning I spotted him feeding a bowl of sticky red rice to the pigeons. I wasn't sure whether I should say something or not. Food left lying on the street attracted not only pigeons but rats too. It was a major problem in some parts of the city. Apparently, the pigeons were not so bad — your pet budgie was more likely to make you ill — but the rats, they were really dirty. They ran through the gutter at night and some of them were over a foot long, not counting the tail. However, I didn't want to behave like a busybody neighbour and start telling him off. Maybe his religion required him to feed the animals. Or maybe he just loved animals. Like the nice old man in the park who was always feeding the ducks even though everyone knew it wasn't good for their health. Whenever I saw him shaking the last crumbs out of the bag, I never went up to him to say, 'Didn't you know that bread is actually really bad for ducks?'

The man seemed to be avoiding eye contact. Because he felt embarrassed? Or because he was shy? Or maybe because I was a woman. I wondered if he had come to the Netherlands as a refugee. And if he was from Somalia; his face had the same soft roundness to it as his son's. I had never seen a woman going into or out of the house. Maybe his wife had to stay indoors? Would it be possible to speak to her? And, most importantly, did the family have liability insurance? Did I even have my own children's names on our insurance policy?

When one of my sons knocked a man down while skating at the local ice rink — at the time he was only three and I still don't know how he managed it, baby skates and all — the man livid, his expensive new selfie-stick all bent — our insurance covered everything.

'That's the end of that so,' the owner of the scooter said, staring down the street.

'It'll be all right,' I said. 'Tell you what. I'll go and get them. Nikola, want to come with me?' We crossed the busy shopping street together and walked down the next street to the house with the sumac tree.

As if by some miracle, the door slowly opened. And out he came, the man with the gentle eyes. See.

'I'm glad you're in,' I said cheerfully. 'There's been an accident, but no one's been hurt.'

He looked worried, his son standing behind him like a silent shadow.

'He kicked it, it wasn't me.' Nikola pointed at Bilal.

'Shut your mouth!' shouted his mother, who had come click-clacking along after us, with the Moroccan man following behind her pushing his battered scooter.

The father looked at us but said nothing, his arms across his chest. Was he silently burning with rage? Or had he experienced such terrible things on his journey to the Netherlands that nothing really fazed him any more?

His silence infected everyone else, each person quietly adopting a hostile attitude.

'My bike fell against a van once and the insurance paid for everything,' I said, trying to sound upbeat. 'It was no trouble at all.'

No one said a word. The man had parked his scooter in the middle of a wide section of the pavement. On the same street there was a car-cleaning service called Perfect Polish, where only very expensive cars went for a shine. With a theatrical flourish of his arm, he pointed at the damage to the scooter and gave Bilal's father a steely look.

'Tell your father what happened,' I said to Bilal, who kept his eyes firmly on the ground.

Nikola: 'We were just passing the ball to each other and then the man came along on the scooter all of a sudden.'

'You're not blind, are you?' said the Moroccan.

'It's only a scratch,' Nikola's mother said sharply.

'There's quite a bit of damage,' I said. 'But you will be fully reimbursed.'

Bilal's father gave me a questioning look. I tried to read his mind; was he insured?

'Give me a minute,' he said, and he disappeared back inside, closing the door behind him.

The man took out his telephone and made a call. In a moment there would be a gang of heavies on the scene making threats; there might even be a fight.

'Fell... all smashed up... yeah... I'm on the Lusthofstraat, near the fat coolie, you know the place.'

I could only hope that the man who was polishing the rims on a Mercedes down the street hadn't overheard him.

'He's on his way,' said the young man after he had hung up.

'Who?' I asked. 'If you just exchange details, no one will need to come.'

He kept his eyes on the end of the street.

'Don't forget to take a photo of the damage,' I said nervously, 'for the insurance. Did you take one when the scooter was lying on the ground?'

He just crossed his arms and said nothing.

A black Volkswagen came around the corner. That'll be them. Almost simultaneously, Bilal's father emerged from the house. Calm as you like, as if he had all the time in the world. But no sign of a folder or piece of paper in his hand.

A slightly older-looking Moroccan man parked his car on the pavement and stepped out. He ignored us and went over to his brother, cousin, friend and placed a hand on his shoulder. 'What's up, bro?'

The young man told him the whole story — with steam coming out of his ears.

'Relax,' said his friend, before turning to me and saying, 'He just got that scooter, you know.'

And then, that's when I thought: now's the moment, now they're going to start making threats, demanding that it be settled here and now, that the cash be handed over, or else. But then he pulled a white form from the Louis Vuitton bag that was strung across his shirt.

He gave it to me. It was a claim form, the standard kind. For Bilal's father. When I went to hand it over, he held up his telephone. In all my anxiety, I hadn't noticed him standing there waiting to show it to me. I read the name of his bank on the screen and then the words 'Liability Insurance' followed by his name and the names of his children: BILAL SALEH, 17-01-2010 and CUMAR SALEH, 18-04-2006. There was no mention of a mother.

'Accidents can happen,' said the friend. 'Just fill in the form and we're done.' He smiled. 'That's the way we do things here in the Netherlands.'

'Are you familiar with this form?' I asked Bilal's father.

'Of course,' he said. And then, just as I was beginning to feel completely useless, he added, 'Could you fill it in for me?'

'Yes. Sure,' I said. 'I don't know anything about scooters, but I'm good at writing.' I wondered if I was to write an account of everything that had taken place outside my house, would it make a good story? Did I know these people well enough to be able to mould them into credible and complex characters? And what was the plot exactly?

I outlined the incident on the form and I described how the damage had been caused by a football and not by another vehicle.

'Now all you have to do is call the insurance company and they will take care of everything.' I looked at Bilal's father and then at the other men. 'Do you understand? The insurance will sort it out. The whole lot.'

They nodded. Bilal hadn't budged an inch the whole time; I had almost forgotten he was there. Nikola was on the other side of the street yanking on a young acacia that had only recently been planted. His mother was busy on her phone.

'Hey,' I said. 'Be careful with that tree.'

The claim form was handed around in triplicate on the pavement before me. The men shook hands and the friend jumped in his car and drove off.

'Well, I guess I should be going too.' I waved but no one noticed, as far as I can recall anyway. Father and son had shuffled back inside the house and the young man was already pushing his scooter down the street. Back to the lease company maybe? Would the scooter genuinely not start for him? Or was this just all part of the show?

I walked back home together with Nikola's mother. Nikola ran on ahead of us. He found his ball, which he had hidden under a car, and began bouncing it on the road. The sun had come out and was bringing out the colours of the roofs of the cars parked in our street. It looked like it was going to be a beautiful day.

PLASTIC MAN

At the roundabout, I turn my back on the city and walk into the woods. Past the fountain with the salamander and the fluted, red stone basin, where I often wash myself or my clothes, and then on down Pheasant Lane, deeper into the trees.

I avoid the light as much as possible. I like to stick to the shadows, to move among the old beeches, standing tall on their statuesque trunks, blocking out the light with their crowns.

Beech tree trunks are smooth, unlike willows with their brittle bark and hollows. Willows offer lots of hiding places. Beeches are slippery customers.

The evening is muggy and hot. The smell of mud hangs in my nose. It is a scent I love — leaves, insects, humus. A little cloud of flies hovers above the path. I swish them away and pace out seventeen steps from the bench. When I reach the trail marker, I leave the path and push on through beds of leaves, over the ditch, past the clump of elderberry bushes in the last throes of bloom. Soon they will be full of fruit with which I will stuff my mouth; bitterly sour but OK with a bit of sugar. Empty café terraces are great for stocking up on a few sachets. I always make sure to snatch a handful from the saucers before the staff can spot me.

My things are stashed under the thick trunk of a fallen ash. Ash trees are not very sturdy. I brush away the dead leaves. Woodlice run for cover. The sweet smell of decay. I pull at a piece of plastic and extract a flat package from the gap under the trunk. My fold-up house.

I hear a cry from the path. Has someone seen me? I look around quickly. A father is hoisting his little missy up onto his shoulders. A boy walks beside them, dragging a scooter behind him, longing for a strip of tarmac he can zip around on. I prefer the soft earth and the bed it offers me.

Their voices bounce around among the trunks of the old beeches. The father lets the girl tilt to one side, pretends to let her fall, and then straightens up again. She sits on his shoulders like a duchess, roaring with laughter. I keep myself hidden behind the elderberry bushes. Before long they'll be heading back home to sleep by their nightlights. Children often get a fright when they see me.

In the summer, I go to bed late. I prefer to wait until dark before heading deeper into the woods. I stay as far away as possible from nocturnal activity. From the drunk students who go skinny-dipping in the lake. From the men looking for other men. From the shady business.

When the weather is bad, I walk along the lakeside. When it is good, like today, I stick to the quiet paths and laneways. I stuff the package under my arm. The plastic has begun to turn green, slowly but surely I am becoming wood, am of the wood. Tramps smell of moss. There's nothing wrong with that, fluffy moss softens everything.

It won't be dark for another hour or two. I fold open the sheet of plastic and wrap it around my shoulders. I follow a horse trail deeper into the trees. I am afraid of barbecuers, night drinkers, couples making out on the benches. They might report me. And dogs, big dogs with wet noses and sharp teeth who are very good at sniffing me out.

Once a man asked me what I was doing here. Once a man asked me whether I had a house. Once a man told me to clear off. Once a man said I didn't belong here. Once a man offered to help me. Once a man threw a stone at me. Once a man came along with a dog that bit me. Once a man took a piss at a tree next to where I was sleeping. The pungent stench found its way into my nostrils.

It was a woman who called the police. I spent that night indoors.

Last winter there was a body in the stream behind the deer park. I saw it floating there. Facedown. It was a man in a beige jacket. The jacket was a balloon. His hands were grey and swollen. His hair fanned out from his head. I used a stick to push him towards the path. The park ranger knows who I am. I remove broken birdhouses from the tree trunks. When he's not around I leave dead animals at his shed. Fallen trees I mark with an orange ribbon.

When it freezes I sleep at the Salvation Army. Only when there's no other option. Sometimes they give me a hot meal. Always cauliflower, like it's the only vegetable on earth. When they try to talk to me I keep my silence.

Twilight is falling, the birds are still singing, high up in the trees. I know that birds are dinosaurs. They survived the Great Catastrophe at the end of the Cretaceous. To survive, the birds had to become smaller. I imagine myself climbing up through the branches, unfolding my plastic wings, higher. I am not a bird. My head is much too big.

Sometimes I want to leave the city and go and live in a bigger wood, like the Schwarzwald in Germany, or among the holm oaks in Spain. But I don't think I could live so far away from other people. I dream of cushions of moss, but I eat out of dustbins.

On hot days the woods smell of grilled meat and charcoal fires. I check all of the bins, one by one. I know which ones have the most to offer. On hot days they overflow, horns of plenty.

Later, when all the dogs are in their baskets, when all the nocturnal tourists have gathered in their secret places, all the men looking for men. Later, when everyone is gone, I sit out on the jetty on the lake and watch the city. It gives off so much light that there are never any stars here. Someday I will go to a place where there are stars.

nieuw new
dutch **nederlands**
stemmen voices

VERZET is a series of chapbooks showcasing the work of some of the most exciting writers working in Dutch today, published by Strangers Press, part of the UEA Publishing Project.

Each story is beautifully translated and presented as an individual chapbook, with a design inspired by the text in collaboration with The Dutch Foundation for Literature and National Centre for Writing.

1 **RECONSTRUCTION**
   by Karin Amatmoekrim trans. by Sarah Timmer Harvey

2 **THANK YOU FOR BEING WITH US**
   by Thomas Heerma van Voss, trans. by Moshe Gilula

3 **BERGJE**
   by Bregje Hofstede trans. by Alice Tetley-Paul

4 **THE TOURIST BUTCHER**
   by Jamal Ouariachi trans. by Scott Emblen-Jarrett

5 **RESIST! IN DEFENCE OF COMMUNISM**
   by Gustaaf Peek trans. by Brendan Monaghan

6 **THE DANDY**
   by Nina Polak trans. by Emma Rault

7 **SHELTER**
   by Sanneke van Hassel trans. by Danny Guinan

8 **SOMETHING HAS TO HAPPEN**
   by Maartje Wortle trans. by Jozef van der Voort

Supported by
N National Centre for Writing
N ederlands letterenfonds dutch foundation for literature

This series was made possible by generous funding from The Dutch Foundation for Literature